45 P

The Young World Library is a series designed for the young reader. The stories are taken from some of the world's best-known novels, plays, legends, operas and ballets. They have been simplified and re-told in a way which keeps close to the spirit of the original, while bringing everything within the immediate grasp of the young reader's understanding of words. Equally important are the illustrations, which have been chosen both to delight the eye and to match the special character of each story. Thus the Young World Library offers young readers a unique stepping stone towards the use and enjoyment of books. It also introduces them in a lively, up-to-date way to many famous stories and characters from the wonderful world of literature and the performing arts.

Series Editor: Alan Blackwood

© 1974 Thomas Nelson & Sons Limited.
SBN 72381028 1
Printed in Great Britain by A. Wheaton & Co., Exeter.

THE
QUEEN'S SECRET

Adapted and told by
Marjorie Hichisson

Illustrated by
Terry Burton

Based on the novel *The Three Musketeers* by
Alexandre Dumas

Jonas D'Artagnan lived in a
village in France. He had
always wanted to be a soldier.
One day he said to his parents:
"I'm going to Paris to join
the King's Musketeers. They
are the finest soldiers in
all France!"

Jonas saddled his horse.
Then he kissed his mother,
shook hands with his father,
waved to his brothers and
sisters, and set off for Paris.

That evening, tired and hungry,
Jonas stopped at an inn. As
he entered, he noticed three
gaily dressed Musketeers sitting
at a table drinking wine.

"What wonderful luck," Jonas
thought. "I will present myself
to them."

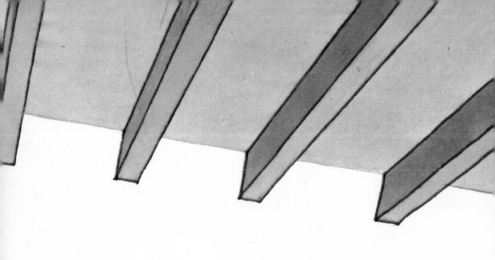

Just then there was a great
clattering of horses in the
yard outside. Another band
of soldiers rushed into the room.

"By heavens, the Cardinal's
men!" one of the Musketeers cried.
"On guard, my friends. One for
all, and all for one!"

Jonas didn't stop to think.
He drew his sword and fought
side by side with the three
Musketeers. Tables and chairs
were overturned. A lamp came
crashing down from the rafters.

At last the Cardinal's men
were forced back through the
door of the inn. One lay
wounded in the yard. The
others jumped onto their horses
and galloped off.

13

"Well done, young man," one of
the Musketeers said to Jonas.
"You helped us out of a tricky
spot. Pray tell me your name."

"Jonas D'Artagnan, sir," Jonas
answered proudly.

"Allow me to introduce myself,"
the Musketeer continued.

"My name is Aramis. And these are my comrades, Athos and Porthos."

"The Three Musketeers!" Jonas exclaimed. "The most famous soldiers in all France."

Aramis smiled. "I believe we have that honour," he said.

"Who were the men who attacked you just now?" asked Jonas.

Aramis told him they were soldiers employed by Cardinal Richelieu.

"Cardinal Richelieu is a very powerful man," Athos added. "Some say he wants the throne of France for himself. Lately he has been plotting against the Queen. If he can harm her reputation this will be bad for King Louis himself."

"We have a secret letter from
the Queen," Porthos explained.
"We have orders to deliver it
to the Duke of Buckingham in
London. The Queen herself has
told us that the throne of France
may depend upon it."

"We are riding to Calais to
take the boat to England," Aramis
went on. "The Cardinal's men
will do everything they can to
stop us. Ride with us, Jonas.
Soon we may need your help again."

19

The next day Jonas and the Three
Musketeers set off for Calais.
As they were riding through a
forest, Aramis suddenly shouted:
"Look out!"

One of the Cardinal's soldiers
jumped down from a tree and pulled
Porthos from his horse. Other
soldiers jumped down after him.

"All for one, and one for all,"
shouted Athos, as he, Aramis and
Jonas went to the rescue of their
comrade.

The Cardinal's men were put to
flight, but Porthos had hurt
his leg.

"Don't stop for me," he told
the others. "The Queen's letter
is more important than anything
else in the world. Ride on.
There's no time to lose!"

Jonas, Aramis and Athos rode like
the wind. They galloped across
wide plains, through dark woods,
and clattered through towns and
villages. They splashed through
a river.

"On guard, my friends," Athos
shouted. "The Cardinal's men
again."

Athos rode straight into the
group of soldiers waiting on the
other bank. Jonas and Aramis came
to his aid as fast as they could.

Again they won, but now Athos was injured.

"Here Aramis," he said. "You take the Queen's letter. The boat for England sails on the midnight tide."

"You and young D'Artagnan must
not miss it. See, it's getting
dark already."

At last Jonas and Aramis saw
the lights of Calais ahead of
them. "Not far now," Aramis
said.

They galloped through the
cobbled streets and reached the
quayside. Suddenly, out of the
darkness appeared two more of
the Cardinal's men. They ran
at Aramis, and one of them landed
a blow on his arm. He fell to
the ground.

29

30

Jonas fought more skilfully and bravely than ever before. He killed one of the soldiers.

The other ran off into the night.

"Jonas, I am hurt," Aramis said. "Now you must take the Queen's letter to the Duke of Buckingham."

A bell started to chime.

"Midnight!" Jonas cried. He ran towards the boat. Already sailors were pulling up the gangplank.

"Wait! Wait for the Queen's messenger!" Jonas called out. He jumped onto the gangplank and scrambled aboard.

When Jonas arrived in London,
he went straight to the Duke
of Buckingham.

"Allow me to present myself,
sir," he said to the Duke.
"My name is Jonas D'Artagnan,
companion of the Three Musketeers.
I bring you a letter from the
Queen of France. I am told
that the fate of the Queen and
of King Louis depends upon your
answer."

The Duke quickly broke the Queen's seal and read the letter.

"By heavens, you're right," he declared. "When I was in Paris, the Queen gave me a diamond necklace. Now she says that Cardinal Richelieu has heard about the gift. He will make King Louis jealous of me. That could mean war between France and England. Only Richelieu could benefit from such a war. The necklace must be returned to the Queen at once. That way we can still foil the Cardinal's plans."

The Duke of Buckingham gave the precious necklace to Jonas.

"Hurry, Monsieur D'Artagnan," he said. "The honour of the Queen of France and the fate of our two countries now rests with you."

Jonas rode faster than ever back
to Dover, and then from Calais
to Paris. He arrived at the Royal
Palace and ran up the steps.

"I have an urgent package for the
Queen," he told the royal guard.
"Tell Her Majesty it is from the
Duke of Buckingham in England."

As soon as the Queen received
the message, she summoned Jonas
to her private apartments.

"Monsieur D'Artagnan," she
said. "By delivering my letter
to the Duke, and returning with
this necklace, you have saved my
honour and that of your King.
You have been of great service
to France. We invite you to
join the King's Company of
Musketeers."

Jonas bowed low. "Your Majesty
has granted me my greatest
wish," he said.

The next night there was a great
banquet and ball in the palace.
The Queen appeared wearing the
precious necklace. It gleamed
and glittered in the candlelight.

Everyone looked happy, except
Cardinal Richelieu. He bowed to
the King and Queen, then quickly
left the ballroom. Aramis, Athos
and Porthos watched him go.

"He knows when he's beaten,"
Jonas said.

"Yes," Porthos observed. "But
if I know the Cardinal, he'll soon
be up to fresh mischief. So keep
your sword sharp, Jonas my friend!"